GRUMPY BUNNIES

GRUMPY BUNNIES

by Willy Welch
illustrated by Tammie Lyon

Whispering Coyote

A Charlesbridge Imprint

*A **Whispering Coyote** Book*
Published by Charlesbridge Publishing
85 Main Street
Watertown, MA 02472
(617) 926-0329
www.charlesbridge.com

Printed in China
10 9 8 7 6 5 4 3 2 1
The illustrations in this book were done in watercolors.
The display type and text type were set in Ad Lib.
Color separations were made by Toppan Printing.
Printed and bound by Toppan Printing
Book production and design by *The Kids at Our House*

Library of Congress Cataloging-in-Publication Data

Welch, Willy.
Grumpy Bunnies / Willy Welch ; illustrated by Tammie Lyon.
p. cm.
Summary: Grumpy Bunnies have a very busy day getting ready for school, learning
lessons, playing on the playground, snacking on crackers after school, and going to bed.
ISBN 1-58089-053-9 (reinforced for library use)
ISBN 1-58089-060-1 (softcover)
[1. Day—Fiction. 2. Schools—Fiction. 3. Rabbits—Fiction. 4. Stories in rhyme.]
I. Lyon, Tammie, ill. II. Title.

PZ8.3.W44 Gr 2000
[E]—dc21   99-052890

jj Fic

To Wendy, my favorite morning person
—W.W.

For Kaitie—
my niece, my friend, and always my inspiration
—Aunt Tam

**Grumpy Bunnies
in the morning**

crusty eyes and groggy yawns

stumble bumbling in the closet
struggle putting school clothes on

Grumpy Bunnies
chomping breakfast
lumpy oatmeal
soggy bread
slumping in their table places
frumpy faces
sulky heads

Grumpy Bunnies
riding buses
knobby seats on bumpy streets

stomping, trudging on the pavement
scuffy shoes and achy feet

**Grumpy Bunnies
on the playground
jungle gymming**

tossing balls

muddy running

grungy sneakers

coming when the teacher calls

Grumpy Bunnies
munching lunches
yummy crumbs of sandwich things

in their classes
learning lessons
numbers
dancing
songs and sings

Grumpy Bunnies after school

huggy mommy

holding hands

tummies hungry cracker snacking

laps and stories

fairy-lands

Grumpy Bunnies bubble bathing

comfy jammies

silky sheets

tucking blankets snuggly kisses

Grumpy Bunnies go to sleep.

Grumpy Bunnies
snuffle snoring,
flopping in their featherbeds

Grumpy Bunnies
slumber dreaming—

there's another day ahead.